EKA AND THE ELEPHANTS

ONCE UPON A
Dance

ILLUSTRATED BY CRISTIAN GHEORGHITA

Dedicated
to all
animal
lovers.

Eka and the Elephants
A Dance-It-Out Creative Movement Story for Young Movers

© 2022 ONCE UPON A DANCE
Illustrated by Cristian Gheorghita
Based on a story by Leah Irby
All proceeds donated to nonprofits helping elephants

Summary: Dance along with Eka and Ballerina Konora in this interactive adventure. Eka's family planted a garden, but Eka worries that animals will eat all the plants. Can Eka save the vegetables and flowers when a playful elephant visits?

LCCN: 2022907644
ISBN 978-1-955555-47-0 (paperback); 978-1-955555-46-3 (ebook); 978-1-955555-46-3 (hardcover)
Juvenile Fiction: Animals: Elephants
(Juvenile Fiction: Cooking & Food; Interactive Adventures; Imagination & Play; Performing Arts: Dance)

First Edition

Other ONCE UPON A DANCE Titles:
Joey Finds His Jump!: A Dance-It-Out Creative Movement Story for Young Movers
Petunia Perks Up: A Dance-It-Out Movement and Meditation Story
Dayana, Dax, and the Dancing Dragon: A Dance-It-Out Creative Movement Story for Young Movers
Danny, Denny, and the Dancing Dragon: A Dance-It-Out Creative Movement Story for Young Movers
Princess Naomi Helps a Unicorn: A Dance-It-Out Creative Movement Story for Young Movers
The Cat with the Crooked Tail: A Dance-It-Out Creative Movement Story for Young Movers
Brielle's Birthday Ball: A Dance-It-Out Creative Movement Story for Young Movers
Mira Monkey's Magic Mirror Adventure: A Dance-It-Out Creative Movement Story for Young Movers
Freya, Fynn, and the Fantastic Flute: A Dance-It-Out Creative Movement Story for Young Movers
Danika's Dancing Day: A Dance-It-Out Creative Movement Story for Young Movers
Andi's Valentine Tree: A Dance-It-Out Creative Movement Story for Young Movers
Dancing Shapes: Ballet and Body Awareness for Young Dancers
More Dancing Shapes: Ballet and Body Awareness for Young Dancers
Nutcracker Dancing Shapes: Shapes and Stories from Konora's Twenty-Five Nutcracker Roles
Dancing Shapes with Attitude: Ballet and Body Awareness for Young Dancers
Konora's Shapes: Poses from Dancing Shapes for Creative Movement & Ballet Teachers
More Konora's Shapes: Poses from More Dancing Shapes for Creative Movement & Ballet Teachers
Dance Stance: Beginning Ballet for Young Dancers with Ballerina Konora

Hello Fellow Dancer,

My name is Ballerina Konora. I love stories, adventures, and ballet.

I'm glad you're here with me! Will you be my dance partner and act out the story with me and Eka? I've included my movement ideas, but you can create your own moves or use the illustrations for inspiration.

Be safe, of course, and do what works for your body in your space. And you might prefer to settle in and enjoy the pictures the first time through.

ONCE UPON A DANCE, Eka's brother and sister, Koda and Kanoni, designed a garden and invited Eka and their parents to help.

Eka's father dug a trench while Koda turned on the faucet and filled the watering can. Eka's mother held the seeds, and Eka gently plucked and dropped each one into the trench. Kanoni scooped up some dirt and sifted it through her fingers as she covered the seeds.

Let's act out the story along with Eka's family. We'll pretend to dig with the shovel, feeling resistance as we push into the soil. Lift and flip the shovel over to dump the dirt. Use your wrist to turn the faucet handle while you hold the watering can.

Next, pinch your finger and thumb together to pick up the tiny seeds. Squeeze with enough force to hold the seeds without squishing them as you bend over and drop each one on the ground.

Bend your knees and get close to the ground. Reach your hands down into the pretend dirt, scooping it up and letting it fall between your wriggling fingers to cover the seeds like Kanoni.

Eka couldn't wait to see what vegetables would come up and imagined being one of the seeds: quiet and still in the cool earth, reaching roots down deep into the ground.

Each day, Eka watered the plants and checked the ground for signs of life. Eka was concerned nothing had grown, but Kanoni and Koda said, "Just be patient, Eka."

Then, one day, a few specks of green splattered the brown dirt. As they grew, the shoots looked like little green hands waving hello.

Let's enjoy a moment of stillness like the seeds. I'm crouched down on my knees, my body folded forward, with my arms reaching behind me. Can you think of a different way to make a small, closed shape? Imagining my roots reaching into the ground is something I do to calm myself, which helps me be a better dancer.

Bend your knees to get closer to the ground again and pretend to water the plants. How low can you go and still stay balanced? Then be the plant emerging from the soil.

As the plants grew taller, leaves started to appear. The pea plants were Eka's favorite—they had long tendrils, like octopus legs reaching out in all directions. Koda hammered sticks into the ground near the peas, and the plants wrapped themselves around the sticks so they could grow tall and reach toward the sun.

The growing sunflowers, with their leaves launching up and out, reminded Eka of fountains.

A few days later, the pea plants grew white flowers, and soon, little pea pods poked out. The garden was blooming with colors and smelled like spring.

Reach your fingers, elbows, toes, and knees in every direction as you search for something to grab onto. Next, pretend you're Koda pushing the sticks in and hammering them down. Then switch back to being a plant and gently wrap all your limbs around something (or someone).

To grow like a sunflower, sit on your knees and lean forward. Lift your head up so you are taller, but keep your bottom on your knees. Then lift your bottom up so you are even taller. For an extra challenge, try to stand without using your hands. Shoot your leaves up and out like a fountain. Then be a little leaf leaning sideways as the plant grows.

9

When the vegetables were almost ready for picking, Eka noticed footprints in the garden, bites in the cabbage, and a hole in the ground where a carrot had been. "What animal could have made this mess?" Eka wondered.

Luckily, plenty of vegetables remained for Eka's family to enjoy. Eka picked the peas lowest to the ground, washed them, and popped the peas from their pods. Kanoni picked, chopped, and cooked some cabbage, and Koda picked two carrots and cut them into pieces.

Pretend to pick some peas by reaching down and gently twisting the pods from the vine. Then, use your finger and thumb to squeeze the peas from their pods. For the carrots, hold the tops of the plant with a fist and pull while trying to wiggle the carrot out of the ground. Chop the veggies using your flat hand as an imaginary knife.

While Eka's family enjoyed their harvest feast, Koda shared something interesting he'd learned at school. "Did you know elephants can eat seven times as much food, and drink five times as much water, as a human? And elephants don't like bees, even though they're at least a hundred times bigger!"

That night, Eka fell asleep wondering if it was a hungry elephant that had invaded their garden.

Imagine you're eating a delicious feast like Eka's family. When I try something super yummy, I rub my belly and say *mmmm*.

Let's see your elephant and bee impressions. It's amazing how the same body can feel like a heavy, slow elephant or a light, fast-moving bee. And how does it feel to drift off to sleep, your body relaxing into the surface beneath you? If you've read any of my other books, you know how I love to sleep!

Eka woke up to the sound of tapping. Something was knocking on the window. Eka jumped out of bed and pushed aside the curtains to see a purple trunk nudging the glass.

An elephant pushed the window open and tickled Eka's cheek with its trunk. Then, the elephant curled its trunk into a seat and scooped Eka off the ground. Without any warning, Eka flew out the open window, sailed up and over, and landed on the elephant's back. "Whee!" said Eka with a huge grin.

How many taps do you imagine?
Can you make tapping sounds with your body?

Rush to the window like Eka and push the curtains out of the way. Act surprised at what you see.

I'd love to ride an elephant. It would make me want to put my hands in the air and shout a happy *Whee!* My grandma worked at a zoo. I'm a little jealous that my mom used to ride the elephants around the zoo when she was little.

Eka held on tight as the elephant ran toward the neighbor's farm. They stopped at the pond. The elephant used its trunk to suck up some water and sprayed it into its open mouth. Then it sprayed the water up in the air and got Eka all wet!

The elephant ran back to Eka's garden and came to a stop. Eka swung both legs together and slid down to the ground. The elephant leaned sideways, then fell to the ground with a thump and started rolling around. Eka joined in and couldn't stop giggling. Eka wished the elephant could stay as a pet and a friend.

Hmm, a running elephant? Let's try to go fast while leaning over like Eka's elephant. Then, let's drop our trunks into the water and slurp it up like we're sucking yummy juice through a huge straw. Pretend to spray anyone who's in the room with you. ☺ I hope they don't get too wet.

Finally, roll on the ground like the elephant and Eka. Rolling around makes me giggle. What about you?

Suddenly, the elephant stopped and sniffed the air with its mighty trunk. It bolted upright and dashed toward a row of cabbages at the edge of the garden. Dirt and carrot tops flew as the elephant gobbled the cabbages one by one. Then it started on the next row of carefully planted vegetables. Eka jumped, waved, and shouted, but the elephant kept eating. What a mess!

If that wasn't bad enough, the elephant trumpeted, and more elephants came running. Now the garden was full of elephants, pulling up vegetables, eating, and rolling around. Eka realized if they kept going, they'd eat all the vegetables and destroy the garden. Eka didn't know what to do.

```
What a crazy scene.
Be like Eka hollering
and jumping around, then
turn back into a running and then a
rolling elephant. Use your arm as a trunk
and toss cabbages into your elephant mouth.
```

Eka remembered what Koda had said about elephants and had an idea. Eka ran to the kitchen, grabbed a jar of honey, climbed over the fence, and followed the neighbor's driveway toward the beehives.

Eka's neighbor had taught the whole family about bees and how they show each other where to find flowers using a waggle dance. Whether it was Eka's shaking or the honey, the bees followed. As Eka climbed back over the fence, the honey jar slipped and fell on the other side. The bees got upset, and Eka ran back toward the house with bees buzzing angrily behind.

The elephants saw the bees, dropped the vegetables, and took off.

To get over the fence, kick your leg sideways holding your honey jar, then land on that leg with the other leg in the air.

For the waggle dance, first bend one knee at a time so your hips move side to side, then shake all over as fast as possible. Try to keep shaking while you walk forward—that's a tricky one. Sideways leap back over the fence and away from the angry bees. Then, switch-a-roo to be an elephant fleeing in fear.

Desperate to escape the swarming bees and pounding elephants, Eka flung open the front door, slammed it, and slumped down on the other side. Eka panted—chest and shoulders lifting and falling with each breath. Eka checked and was relieved to not find any bee stings.

    Turn the doorknob and fling
    the door open. Quickly step inside
    the house, lean against a wall, and slide down to the
    floor. Take a few deep sighs, lifting your shoulders as you
    breathe in and dropping your shoulders as you breathe out.
    Slide your hands up and down your arms to check for stings.

Happy to be safe inside, Eka lay on the floor with eyes closed. After three slow breaths, Eka stretched and looked around in surprise.

Eka was back in bed! Eka pushed back the covers and ran to the window. The garden was still there, full of vegetables and flowers. A little lone rabbit sat nibbling on a pea plant.

Still feeling dazed, Eka went to find the family at breakfast.

```
        Lie on the ground.
     Slowly breathe in through your
   nose and out through your mouth.
    Then reach out to make yourself longer.
 Try reaching out with flexed hands and feet—sometimes I
 find I can push farther if I pull my fingers and toes back.
 Let's lie on our sides as we act surprised. Then jump out of
 bed like Eka and peek out the window.

 For the rabbit, let's twitch our noses all around, which moves our
 lips more than our noses. Then, let's
                  shake our tail
                  and take a few
                  rabbit hops.
```

"I just had the strangest dream," said Eka. "A lovely elephant came to visit, but then she invited her friends, and they ate all the vegetables in our garden." Eka sighed. "Even though the garden was ruined, I'm sad it wasn't real. I think it would be nice to have an elephant friend. Mom, is there any way we could visit an elephant someday?"

Eka's mom laughed, shook her head, and said, "Honey, I'm sorry, but I don't know any elephants."

Kanoni ran to her room and came back with a picture of an elephant on her tablet. "Look! I saw a place that saves orphaned elephants. You can visit them. Maybe Eka could have an elephant friend after all."

Imagine the scene, and act out each of the characters. How do you think Eka shows excitement? I imagine Eka's mom with hands on hips and tilted head before she shakes her head no. And I think Kanoni would lean forward to show her mom the picture.

Eka's mom thought it was a wonderful idea. A few days later, they went to the sanctuary to visit a young elephant named Juza. Eka sang a song, and the little elephant swayed to the music. Eka and the twins danced, swinging their pretend trunks, and when Eka made a little bow, Juza wrapped her trunk around Eka's arm.

"Juza wants to give you a hug," the elephant's caretaker told them.

Eka hugged Juza's trunk and said, "I'm so happy to have a new friend."

What song would you sing if you could serenade an elephant? Elephants are so big, I might feel a little scared to meet one in person. Let's take our final bow, and if there's not an elephant around for you to hug, give yourself a hug instead!

Thee End!
The End.

(My grandpa
always ended stories
this way, and I like
to share the fun.)

Thanks for being my dance partner.
Until our next adventure
Love,
Konora

WE'D LOVE TO CONNECT

Once Upon a Dance is a mother-daughter team, both happily immersed in the ballet world until March 2020. With an initial plan to publish one book, we've published 25 books with the mission to keep kids moving at home during the pandemic.

The greatest challenge is getting the books in the hands of kids who will enjoy them. With this goal in mind, we donate Dance-It-Out! stories to libraries, dance instructors, and teachers, and donate all proceeds to charity partners.

We check for reviews daily and would be immensely grateful for a kind, honest review from a grown-up on Amazon or Goodreads or a shout-out or follow on social media if you enjoy our books. Thank you!

@Once_UponADance (Instagram)
OnceUponADanceViralDancing (Facebook)

The Dance-It-Out! Collection

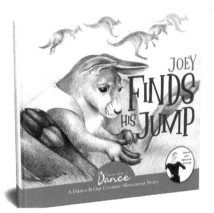

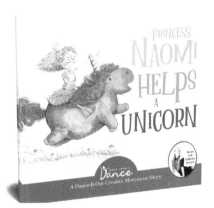

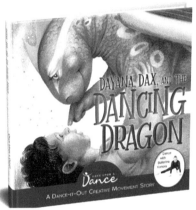

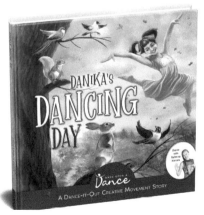

ONCE UPON A
Dance
Series Catalog:
· Dance-It-Out!
· Dancing Shapes
· Konora's Shapes
· Ballet Inspiration

www.Once Upon A Dance.com
Watch for Subscriber Bonus Content

CPSIA information can be obtained
at www.ICGtesting.com
Printed in the USA
BVHW020818271022
650005BV00020B/53